FATAL GESTURE
By JOHN TAINTOR FOOTE

The young couple who were first introduced in the author's perennial favorite, "A Wedding Gift," are again the foils for Mr. Foote's delectable brand of humor. George Baldwin Potter, the husband, is still the passionate and incurable angler whom thousands of readers will at once remember as the man who took his wife fishing on their honeymoon. Now, George is sent to an auction to obtain an antique corner cupboard which his wife is dying to have because she has already secured its mate and has built her dining room around it. Armed with the best of intentions and a catalogue that is carefully marked, George arrives at the auction all right, but gets side-tracked shortly by a remarkable find—a collection of the choicest fishing rods he has ever seen. These are also up for sale. The account of how between testing the rods, talking to the fellow anglers he finds about him, and bidding excitedly against them, his prescribed mission is for a time forgotten is hilariously set forth. Suffice it to say that his horror is increased on learning that his wife's dearest enemy has also had her eye on the cupboard. The results are deliciously humorous and will arouse chuckles and shouts of laughter.

Fatal Gesture

By JOHN TAINTOR FOOTE

Fatal Gesture

By

John Taintor Foote

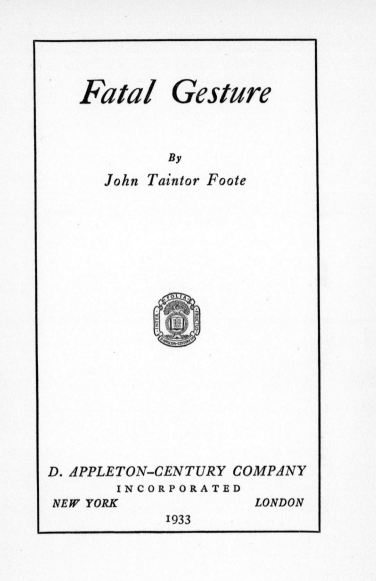

D. APPLETON–CENTURY COMPANY

INCORPORATED

NEW YORK *LONDON*

1933

COPYRIGHT, 1933, BY JOHN TAINTOR FOOTE

b W
.F7393f

Fatal Gesture

Fatal Gesture

SOME ten years or so ago, it was my painful duty to report certain episodes in connection with the marriage and rather brief honeymoon of George Baldwin Potter, passionate angler, and his bride, the fair Isabelle.

From time to time since then, sympathetic readers of the narrative have inquired as to the subsequent relationship of that unfortunate couple.

Such solicitous inquiries have taken, as a rule, the following form: "Did George and Isabelle get together again?" To this question, as the years have passed, I have been able to answer, with increasing satisfaction, in the affirmative.

I have become almost lyrical, I now recall, over the continued felicity of the Potter union. One may judge, therefore, with what misgivings I learned of recent disturbing developments in the domesticity of George and his still-lovely better half.

The indisputable source of my information was George himself. I came upon him skulking—no other word describes it—in the shadows of the deserted club library. Since it was now close to the witching hour of midnight, I looked at him with some astonishment.

"Hello," I said. "What are you doing here?"

He did not return my greeting. Eying me with a sort of furtiveness, I thought, he muttered something unintelligible and attempted to edge from the room in a slinking, unobtrusive manner that suggested burglary or worse.

Now, I had left some excellent pheasant shooting on Long Island and come in to town for the night to attend the début, musically speaking, of a female friend of a female friend. Still simmering with the just wrath which the notes of the incipient songbird had brought to a boil earlier that evening, I seized George roughly by the arm.

"Why are you sliding around here in the dark like a crab?" I demanded. "What's the matter with you, anyway?"

George collapsed into a leather lounge chair with a groan. "Why do I always run into you," he inquired, "at times like these?" He groaned again, but sat erect to favor me with a brooding stare. "You're asking me," he said bitterly. "Now I'm asking you. What are you doing here; why should you be snooping around at all hours when a man just wants to be alone?"

"I'm sorry to have forced my way into your private club," I said. "I'm deeply mortified. I blush at admitting it, but I'm spending the night. If you can believe such a thing, I've taken a room here. I hope you'll forgive my—"

Sarcasm seemed wasted on George.

3

"So have I," he interrupted, and added with mournful dignity, "This is now my home."

"Your what?"

"I said, 'my home.' "

"Since when?"

"Since day before yesterday. I have left Isabelle."

"Not really, George!"

He nodded.

"For good?"

"Absolutely!"

"Why?"

George rose from the chair and faced me. "Her mother," he said simply. He lit a cigarette with shaking fingers and repeated, "Her mother."

My irritation of a moment before had fled. "Life," I thought, "never changes. The old, old story! It goes back to the head of the family, crouching, club in hand, at the mouth of the cave."

Aloud I said, "But, George, why let an

interfering old woman, no matter how obnoxious, destroy your—"

"You're all wrong there," said George. "You're barking up the wrong tree. As a matter of fact, she had ptomaine poisoning."

I simply stared.

George grew uneasy under my eye. "Damn it all," he said, "I suppose I'd better tell you everything! Let's go up to one of our rooms. I have a bottle of Scotch."

"Make it your room," I said.

An elevator bore us aloft. George unlocked a door and snapped on a light. We entered.

There are, no doubt, drearier abiding places on Manhattan Island than its various club bedrooms, but I have not, as yet, been forced to occupy one of them. I was able to take in the furnishings of George's sleeping quarters at a glance. Its general color scheme was a corpselike gray, warmed only by a variegated cataract of neckties wedged between the dresser mirror and its support.

5

On the dresser were two ebony brushes, a comb and one peculiarly significant item. It was Isabelle's picture in a tooled-leather frame. She was smiling.

Gazing at the picture and uplifted by the implication of this face beaming upon George dressing, George undressing, George slumbering through the night, I now assumed a manner indicative of gayety and cheer.

"You old mud turtle," I said, nudging him in the side, "you certainly have a lovely wife."

George dashed me to earth.

"Had," said he, and turned the picture face down upon the dresser. "You take the chair," he commanded; "I'll sit on the bed. But wait a minute—" He went to the telephone. "Do you want soda or ginger ale?"

"Never mind ordering anything for me," I told him. "Plain water will do."

"Suits me too," said George. He reached under the bed, pulled a traveling bag into view and withdrew a bottle from its interior.

6

"Ought to be a couple of glasses here. . . .
Oh, yes, they're in the bathroom." Presently
he was sitting on the bed staring down into
his glass.

I sipped in expectant silence. "Well?"
said I, at last.

"It's a brownish-yellow thing with shelves,"
said George suddenly. "Below are two doors
with wooden catches. That's all there is to
it. I give you my word, that's all there is
to it. Don't think I'm exaggerating. I could
make one myself out of two—well, maybe
three—dry-goods boxes. What do you think
of that?"

"Nothing as yet, George," I told him
patiently.

"Well, you will before I get through, and
don't you forget it. It's called an Early
American cupboard. It was to go in the
breakfast room. Two of 'em. She had
bought one already. The other was to go at
the other end of the room. She had done
the room over for 'em—new paper, new

7

paint. Yellow walls with Colonial-white woodwork, she said. Think that over. But that's nothing. You may not believe me, but it's the truth as God is my judge. She was going to have a perfectly good hardwood floor ripped out and wide boards with knots laid in place of it. I had it from her own lips. Wide boards with knots, was what she said.

"I remember asking her, 'Why knots?' To show you I had perfect control over myself, I laughed when I said it. I laughed and said, 'Pretty good, eh, darling—why nots?' Can I take it? I'll say I can.

"She didn't laugh. She didn't explain about the knots. She put her head on one side, then she put it on the other. She said, 'George, can you imagine what the delft plates are going to look like on those warm yellow shelves against the mustard-colored walls?' "

George paused and slowly shook his head. "Well, I suppose life is like that," he said,

8

and paused again to stare unseeingly at the floor.

"But, George," I said, "somehow I'm not getting this straight in my mind. Somehow I don't seem to get anything from what you are saying. Downstairs you told me it was Isabelle's mother. Where does she come in?"

"She'll come in all right. She'll come in plenty. . . . Where was I?"

"Frankly, George, I don't know."

"Well, what was I talking about?"

"I think," I said cautiously, "that cupboards had something to do with it."

"Something to do with it! I'll tell the cock-eyed world! They had everything to do with it."

"Well, then," I said, "suppose we start with cupboards. Begin right there."

"But, my God," said George, "I've been all over that once."

"My fault, no doubt, but it isn't altogether clear to me even now. Suppose you get this

9

cupboard business straightened out for me. She had two cupboards—was that it?"

"It was not," said George firmly. "She never had two. She had one. I said so distinctly. I'll say it again. She had exactly one cupboard. One—count 'em—cupboard. C-u-p-b-o-r-d—cupboard. Have you taken that in?"

"You left out the '*a*' in cupboard," I said.

"I don't care what I left out, so long as I get it through your thick head that she had one of 'em."

"Don't get excited, George," I said.

George set his glass down on the small table beside the bed and threw his arms despairingly in the air. "I give up," he said. "I give up completely. I've lost my wife. You force yourself into the one home I have left, and when I try to tell you, as a friend— as a friend, mind you—coolly, calmly, clearly, exactly what happened, you sit there drinking my Scotch and tell me I'm excited. I simply give up."

"Don't give up, George," I urged. "I've had a trying day, what with one thing and another. I suppose my mind isn't all it should be. Make allowances for me and go ahead, like a good fellow. First, if you don't mind, just skim over this cupboard business again. Where did she get them—it, I mean."

George eyed me dubiously but went on.

"She got the one cupboard—one, mind you —from old Mrs. Touchard, up in Connecticut. The depression had the old lady on the ropes. She was selling her furniture a piece at a time. She'd part with an old, rickety chair that you couldn't sit in three minutes without dislocating your spine, as though it were her life's blood, and live on the money until it was gone. Then she'd let go of a sort of curlicue bed. Isabelle called 'em— let's see—thread beds? . . . No, that isn't it. . . . Rag beds? . . . No, that's the messy sort of rugs they go crazy over."

"Spool," I suggested.

George looked at me admiringly. "I guess

11

the old bean isn't so dead, after all," he said. "Now, how did you guess that?"

"One of them," I confessed, "severed diplomatic relations between two branches of my family."

"That's it!" said George. "You're beginning to get the idea. Well, listen. Did you ever happen to see a picture I saw once? It was an old buffalo standing in the snow. All around him were wolves, just sitting there waiting for him to topple over. Well, the women Isabelle trains with were like that about old Mrs. Touchard. They just waited. They knew every stick of furniture she had. They'd argue about who was to get what. When the old lady had to sell something, there was a riot.

"I think Isabelle was the leader of the pack. She simply lived at the old lady's. She took her port wine—six bottles, pre-Volstead, I had left—until it was gone. She took her jelly and soup and cold chicken. Once I said, 'Listen, darling; your system's all haywire. Just take her cocktails as an appetizer, and let it go at that.' She said I was heartless and disgusting. That's what you get when you try to help a woman."

George broke off, reached for his glass and drank deeply.

"Well, maybe I was wrong, because Isabelle got the prize package. It was this cupboard I told you about six or seven times. Mrs. Touchard had two of them, exactly alike, and Isabelle got one. The rest of the women would hardly speak to her after she told 'em. She sent it somewhere to have it waxed—I think she said—and started in doing over the breakfast room. She said, 'I'm planning the room for both of them, George; one at each end.' I said, 'How do you know you'll get the other?' She said, 'That's what those silly women are being so absurd about.' Then she told me she'd called a meeting and persuaded the crowd to enter into a ladies' agreement that if any of them got one cupboard, it would be a sort of option on the other. She said, 'You see, they're companion pieces, George; they simply have to go together. They all saw how reasonable and fair my suggestion was at the time.' I said, 'Well, then why are they so snooty about it now?' Isabelle said, 'It's all that Grace Witherbee's doings—the cat.' She wouldn't say anything more for awhile, but at last she told me—well, not told me, exactly; I sort of got it out of her—that Tom Witherbee's wife had found out that Mrs. Touchard had already promised Isabelle one cupboard when Isabelle called the meeting. Can you possibly beat that?"

"What did you say?" I asked.

"Not much," said George. "I didn't get a chance. When I suggested—just suggested, mind you—that the transaction might be—well, a bit shady—she went all to pieces. She said, among other things, that it was simply business. That's what she said—simply business. She said I made her sick. She said I did things at the office like that right along

14

and thought it was clever, but that when my wife showed a little foresight—that's what she called it, 'a little foresight'—I talked like the Sermon on the Mount. Then she went up to her room and locked the door, and when I tried to get in, I heard her weeping. . . . How about another snifter?"

"Not yet," I said. "Go ahead!"

"Well, the unexpected happened. Old Mrs. Touchard died. I asked Isabelle if she thought losing the cupboard killed her, and Isabelle didn't even smile. Funny thing about women—you may have noticed it— absolutely no sense of humor. The old lady died without any warning. They simply found her in the morning. Isabelle had to bring back some pound cake, I think it was, she'd taken up to her. Isabelle said, 'It's such a shame. She adored cake. What on earth am I going to do now?' I said, 'About what?' She didn't answer. She asked a question instead. She said, 'What do they do about estates?' Now, I ask you to try and answer that one. I started in to straighten it out. I said, 'To begin with, who are they?' Isabelle said, 'They are whoever does whatever they do.' I said, 'Darling, that doesn't even begin to make sense.' Isabelle said—I'll give you her exact words—she said, 'George, I wonder if there is anyone else like you anywhere? I wish there was—I'd love so to meet his wife.'" George paused reflectively. "After what's happened," he said at last, "I keep going over things she's said lately, in my mind. I've wondered about the remark I've just repeated to you. What do you make of it?"

"If you don't mind," I said, "I think I'll have that drink you offered me a minute ago, now."

"Why, sure," said George, reaching for the bottle. . . . "Where was I?" he wanted to know, when our glasses were filled.

"She'd asked you about estates."

"Right-o! I found out what she was driving at a week or so later. The executor sent

16

what was left of Mrs. Touchard's furniture to an auction company here in New York, to be sold under the hammer. Isabelle found out the day it was to be sold, and that was that. She put a ring around the date on her desk calendar, and she'd go into the breakfast room, right while the painters or paperhangers were at work, and stand by the hour. The day before the sale she got a sales catalogue from the auction people. She was sitting in the living room that evening, poring over the catalogue, when the telegram came. A maid brought it to her on a tray." George lapsed into silence. He stared down into his glass for a moment, then looked up haggardly at me. "I can see that telegram on the silver tray now," he said. "I can see her take it and tear it open. Little did I think that—" He broke off, was silent for a moment, then raised his glass. "Here's to life," he said, adding, with the glass at his lips, "and a hell of a mess it is."

I joined him in a toast that left him with a

beaded brow and an expression that marked him as one of the doomed.

"Nothing," I offered weakly, "is ever as bad as it seems."

George snorted in derision.

"Oh, is that so?" he said. "Well, listen! The wire was from her father. I've still got it somewhere. It said: 'Your mother ill. Wants you. Come at once.' That's what it said. That's what it said exactly. What do you think of that?"

"I don't know what to think yet," I told him. "Suppose you—"

"Hah!" George burst out. "You don't, eh? Well, you will, I promise you that. Get this: It meant she had to go to New Rochelle that night. It meant she'd have to be there all the next day. All the next day, mind you. Now what do you think?"

"Why, George," I confessed, "I've been to New Rochelle once—I stayed a whole week-end, as a matter of fact. I don't see why she couldn't stand it for—"

"You're right," George broke in. "There is something the matter with your head. Well, try and take this in: The other cupboard was to be sold at auction the next day. Now think this over. Of all the days in the year—in nine years, when you get right down to it—that was the day her mother picked out to have ptomaine poisoning."

I remained speechless.

George rushed on: "While a maid was packing a bag for Isabelle, she told me what I had to do. The cupboard was No. 827 in the catalogue. It would be sold, she said, somewhere around four o'clock next day. But she said not to take a chance. She said something might happen to advance the hour. She said, 'George, the sale starts at two. You be there at one o'clock and simply stay right there until they put it up.' I said, 'Darling, surely you don't expect me to sit there twiddling my thumbs from one o'clock until four?' Isabelle said, 'I didn't know that even you would talk about thumb twiddling.

19

I didn't know any one had ever mentioned it since Thackeray or Dickens. I never asked you to do a single important thing before, and now, when I do, with my own mother dying, for all you know, you bring up thumb twiddling.' Well, of course, that settled it. I told her I'd be there at one o'clock, and she told me to find the cupboard as soon as I got there and then keep my eye right on it until it was put up for sale. How would you like to sit and watch a cupboard for three hours? Now, as man to man, how would you?"

George paused momentarily, but was off again before I was equal to a reply.

"I told her I'd do it. That's exactly what I told her. I want you to notice that in this whole business I never crossed her once. Her wish was my law. That makes what finally happened all the more— But never mind that now. I not only said I'd keep an eye on the cupboard, I also promised I'd top the bid of Grace Witherbee or any of the rest of them, if it took my entire bank balance. And listen; this isn't 1929. I expect even you scribbling fellows know that."

"Yes, George," I said, "we do."

"Well, it only goes to show my attitude. It ought to be clear to you by now that I was for the little woman, lock, stock and barrel, let the tail go with the hide, hook, line and sinker." A spasm swept George's face like a passing cloud at his last metaphor. "Just imagine," he said, "fishing with a sinker. Imagine plopping such a thing into a stream. And yet, up on the Ausable, one day—" George's expression changed. The anxious look left his face, the rigidity went out of his figure. He settled himself comfortably on the bed. "I'll simply have to tell you this. It's really good. I was fishing the ski-jump pool. I was using a No. 12 fan wing, Royal Coachman—early in the day for it—still that's what I was using, I remember. I'd hooked a small native and was taking him off when I saw what looked like a good fish rise about thirty—well, perhaps, thirty-five—

yards above me, close to a rock on the right-hand side of the stream. The native had messed up the fan wing some. I was drying the fly before working up slowly to where I'd seen the rise, when a fellow came out of the bushes just above me, carrying—think this over—a steel rod with a hunk of lead about as big as a—"

"George," I interrupted, "if you get started on that sort of thing, we'll be here all night."

"Eh?" said George, as though returning suddenly from another world. "What did you say?"

I repeated my previous comment.

George sighed.

"All right, all right," he said. "I was only going to relate a— But as you say, perhaps this isn't the time for— Where was I?"

"You'd promised Isabelle to be at the auction rooms by one o'clock."

"Precisely; and, believe it or not, I was there at quarter past. The first thing I did

22

was to locate the cupboard. Naturally, I expected to be knocked dead by it. I had it in my mind's eye as a sort of massive, shiny thing, with carving all over it. I poked around until I came to something with No. 827 pasted on it. I took one look at it and went straight to a young man who seemed to be in charge. I said, 'I'd like to call your attention to a mistake.' He was a pale, thin, unpleasant young man, with light hair and sort of pinkish eyes. He said, 'Really. What sort of a mistake?' I said, 'Oh, nothing very serious. If you'll follow me I'll show you.' I took him over to the thing I'd found and pointed to the number in my catalogue. Isabelle had marked a heavy ring around the number and then underscored 'Early American Cupboard' three times. I said, 'You see?'

"The pale young man looked at the number. His eyebrows went up in a most extraordinary way. You'd hardly believe it— they seemed to go right up into his hair. He said, 'Really, I'm afraid I don't.' I began to get annoyed. I said, 'What kind of a place is this, may I ask?' Then I explained patiently that 827 called for an Early American cupboard. The young man said, 'Quite so,' and stood looking at me with his eyebrows up. I said, 'But damn it all, you've got the number on this thing here.' He said, 'Quite so,' again. Then he ran his hand down the thing I'd found and said, 'Absolutely authentic; about 1780. One of the finest pieces we have ever handled.' He let down his eyebrows and went away. I suppose I stood and took in the Early American cupboard for ten minutes. I've told you what it was like. I tried to figure out why on earth any one would give it house room. I gave up and went and sat in one of the camp chairs that were standing in rows from the front to the back of the place. . . . Cigarette?"

"Thanks," I said, helping myself from his proffered case.

"Drink?"

24

"Not yet."

George lit a cigarette and inhaled deeply.

"Have you ever," he wanted to know, "been in one of these auction rooms?"

"Not that I remember."

"Well, it's depressing," George told me. "So much old furniture and knickknacks and whatnots all around, and the rows of camp chairs and the kind of pulpit thing up front. There were only a few people there—mostly old men with milkish whiskers and thin old women with lorgnettes—poking about and looking at the things that were going to be sold, and not making a sound. I'll say to you I never wanted a drink more in my life. I'd have given ten bucks for a good, stiff pick-me-up. I'd have given fifty if I'd had a flask with me.

"I got out my pipe and started to fill it, but the pale young man, who had been keeping an eye on me in an annoying manner, came and said, 'Sorry, no smoking.' So I just sat there sucking on the empty pipe.

25

"And now get ready for the most surprising thing you ever heard. I had begun to
look through the catalogue just to keep from
rushing out to a speak-easy, and all of a sudden I read: 'Consignment of rods and fishing
tackle. Estate of the late Andrew B. Jenks.'
That is exactly what I read, no more, no less.
Can you believe it?"

"I don't see why not, George," I said.
"What's so surprising about that?"

"Plenty," George told me. "In the first
place, I would have expected to find fishing
tackle at the morgue quicker than where I
was. In the second place, I'd never heard of
Andrew B. Jenks. I still don't understand
that. Not in view of what followed. I remember actually smiling, after my first shock
of surprise, at what the rods and tackle of
Andrew B. Jenks would be like. Yes, sir,
actually smiling." George looked at me and
shook his head. "Pride goes before a fall,"
he said, and helped himself to more Scotch.
"I think of that smile," he presently con-

26

fessed, "with humility and shame; but I've got to admit it. I'm telling you now, I once smiled with contempt at the rods and tackle of Andrew B. Jenks." He drank deeply, placed his glass on the table and again shook his head. "I said I'd tell you everything."

I nodded.

"Well, believe me, I am. I hate to admit what I thought next. I thought: 'After all, I haven't anything else to do. Why not go and look the stuff over?' That was exactly the condescending attitude I took. I'll say that's making a clean breast of it. Of course, you know Spinoza is dead?"

"Why, yes, George, I think I do. He died in sixteen seventy something, wasn't it? At—"

"I suppose you're trying to be funny," George broke in. "I'm not talking about that one—whoever he was. I'm talking about Spinoza the rod maker. He's been dead seven years. Of course, the business has been carried on. A son of the old man

27

is in charge. As a matter of fact, they still put out the best rods on the market, but the rods made by the old man himself have something—well, it's hard to explain. They're just different. You simply know, when you get one in your hand, that you've got hold of the sweetest thing that ever shot a line. Not too whippy, not too stiff, sensitive tip with plenty of backbone in the middle, handle heavy fish for years and years and keep straight as a string. Oh, man, those old Spinozas! I've got nine of 'em—no, ten, now—I'll come to that. I'm simply getting you prepared a little for what happened.

"I went over to where I saw the pale young man and said, 'Where are these so-called fishing rods you're selling here to-day?' His eyebrows went up again. He said, 'The Jenks consignment is in the rug room at the right. We've been informed that it is a particularly fine collection.' I don't know why this fellow irritated me so. It was his eyebrows as much as anything else,

28

I suppose. At any rate, I smiled coldly and said, 'No doubt.' Then I went into the room he had indicated. It was a big room with piles of rugs everywhere you looked. At one end I saw something that startled me. It was a row of leather rod cases standing against the wall—leather, mind you. They ran from one side of the room clear to the other. But that's nothing. That isn't a starter. I went over and began uncasing those rods. Before I'd looked at a dozen I was shaking like a leaf. Listen. You won't believe it, but listen. Every rod I looked at was a Spinoza—made by the old man himself. Every single rod. I remember I thought I was dreaming. There I was alone in that room with forty or fifty old Spinozas. I simply folded up. I had to go and sit down on a pile of rugs. I have never had such a sensation in my life—never.

"I must have sat on that pile of rugs for five minutes just trying to pull myself together. I had sense enough to look in the catalogue and go down the list of rods. Outside of one or two cheap bait rods, everything there was a Spinoza—everything. Light, medium and heavy trout rods. Light, medium and heavy salmon rods. They ran from fairy weight to heavy tournament. I said: 'Oh, my God!' and sat on the pile of rugs staring at the rod cases, for I don't know how long, not thinking especially, just sitting there, sucking on my empty pipe, in a sort of daze. You can imagine the shape I was in. We can only stand so much. A thing like that simply flattens a man.

"After a while I began to think. It began to dawn on me that I was face to face with the chance of a lifetime. It came to me that now I could do something that really counted for the little woman. Get that—for the little woman. That's how my mind was working. How does that strike you?"

"But what had fishing rods to do with Isabelle?" I asked.

"I'll explain it," said George. "It's simply

30

this: No single human being is perfect. Am I right?"

"George," said I, "you are."

"Well, then, I'm going to tell you that I have a—call it a weakness."

"Not really, George?"

"Absolutely!"

"You astound me!"

"It's a fact, just the same. I admit it. I'm not trying to hide it from you. I come right out with it. The fact is, I keep buying fishing rods. Some men drink; some men gamble. I buy fishing rods, and there you are. It has been a constant source of friction between Isabelle and me. Whenever I buy one, I try to slip into the fishing room quietly, without her knowing it. I do it to spare her feelings, naturally. But she has a sort of sixth sense about a new rod. I defy any man to get one into the house without meeting her in the front hall.

"We've had it out dozens of times. At first she used to say, 'But, George, you have heaven knows how many rods now. Why do you buy another one?" That's a hard one to answer. The fact is, I don't know myself. Sometimes when I get home with a rod, I ask myself the same question. But it's too late then. For some years now she doesn't say anything when I come in with one. She just looks at the rod case and then looks at me, while I go past her to the tackle room. Then she goes upstairs and locks herself in her room and stays for hours. Once I said to her, 'Darling, suppose I was a booze fighter, or a woman chaser?' She said, 'Well, that would be more human than this sneaking in with rods. It's queer. It's like taking drugs. It makes me want to scream!' Hell, isn't it? Or, rather, it was. It's all over now." George sighed deeply, drained his glass and lapsed into silence.

"You started to tell me about planning to do something for Isabelle," I urged, at last.

"Yes," said George, coming out of his reverie, "I decided to end my rod buying once and for all. It was certain the old spooks I'd seen in the auction room wouldn't know a Spinoza from a cane pole. I told myself I could buy every rod there for a few dollars each. I thought it all out. Of course, there would be the expense of enlarging the tackle room; but that wasn't to be thought of when you consider what I was doing to spare Isabelle's feelings for years to come. I told myself I'd like to see some slick sporting-goods salesman sell me another rod. I thought I'd let him put it together and wave it in front of my face and then hand it to me. I thought how I'd take it and test it and say, 'Not bad,' and then hand it back to him and march out of the store and go home to Isabelle and my fifty or sixty old Spinozas."

George broke off and indulged once more in rueful head shaking. "Just a dream," he said. "Just an idle dream.

"Well," he went on, "by the time I got back into the auction room, the sale had started. There were a lot more people there by then, all sitting in the camp chairs. Just the same kind of timid-looking old washouts I'd seen before. I sat down in a chair, still in a sort of trance. But pretty soon I got interested in that auctioneer. I don't think I've ever seen any one who impressed me more, at the time. He knew so much, it was simply appalling. It gave you an inferiority complex just to listen to him. No sort of jimcrack could be put up that he couldn't give you the inside facts about. If a Smyrna rug came up, you'd think he'd spent most of his life in Smyrna. The same for Chinese rugs. He knew the province a rug came from like his own back yard. Same about any old rickety piece of furniture. It might be a hundred years old, but he knew the man who made it by his first name, and the day of the week he turned the thing out. There wasn't a corner of the world or a thing in it that could fool him. He'd take a piece of brass, or glass, or china, and glance at it, and that was enough—just a glance and

you'd get the facts as to where it was made,
and when, and what it was worth. And that
wasn't all. He handled the whole thing like
Mussolini. No monkey business; no backing
and filling—just biff, bang, snap! I remember, I thought after a while that here was the
man to lead us out of the depression. I'm
telling you this as a warning. It'll teach you
never to judge a man too hastily. You'll find
out what this fellow turned out to be presently.

"I was awfully cheered by the prices. The
way things were selling was a crime. The
auctioneer said so. They were going, he
said, for a fraction of their value. Judging
by the difference in what he said a thing was
worth and what it sold for, I figured I'd get
my Spinozas for about fifty cents each, case
and all. I remember thinking how strange
life is. There I was, practically the owner of
half a hundred old Spinozas at an outlay of
a few dollars, and I had cursed Isabelle's
mother, earlier that morning, for getting me

into what I thought was a frightful jam. I made up my mind right there I'd invite the old lady to come and stay several days with us—just as soon as I'd got the tackle room enlarged. That'll show you whether or not my heart was in the right place. Why, I know a lot of men who have apoplexy if they hear their wives' mothers are going to spend the night. I'll bet you do too. Now, don't you?"

"Well, something like that," I said.

"There you are," said George. "That goes to show you. Of course, I've got to admit one thing. I've got to admit I didn't think of Isabelle's mother, or Isabelle, for that matter, much longer. But I'll ask you, when you hear what happened, whether you think any man could think of women or their vague, impossible notions at such a time? I'm going to ask you, as man to man, and I want a frank reply. . . . Where was I?"

"You were thinking of having Isabelle's mother for a visit."

"Correct. And right there I got a shock. I hadn't noticed any one come in and sit down, but all of a sudden I realized that there was some one next to me with a pipe in his mouth. I turned like a shot, and there was John Woodruff. The spent-wing Woodruff is named after him. It's a good fly at times. Why, one day over on the Broadhead, I simply couldn't raise a fish. I tried a Cahill first, I think it was—nothing doing. Next I tried a spent-wing Lady Beaverkill— nothing doing. Then I tried a Skews Hackle, No. 14, for twenty minutes or so—nothing doing. Next I tried a—"

"George!" I broke in warningly.

"All right, all right," said George. "Where was I?"

"A man named Woodruff had just—"

"I'll say he had. There he sat. No getting away from it. I could feel the sweat break out on my face. Beyond him was a row of old ladies with lorgnettes, and he sat there with his pipe in his mouth just as

37

though he owned the place. I said, 'Listen. They don't let you smoke in here.' He said, 'Am I smoking?' I said, 'You've got a pipe in your mouth.' He said, 'I've got shoes on my feet but I'm not walking. . . . What are you doing in here?' I told him I had dropped in to see if I could pick up something for the little woman. He said, 'Me, too,' and began to read a catalogue. I tried to see what page he was looking at. But he kept the catalogue tilted away from me. I thought to myself, 'Maybe he doesn't know. Better divert him from that damn catalogue.' So I said aloud, 'Did you hear about the twenty-inch rainbow I took on the East Branch of the Delaware this season?'

"Well, he simply grunted. But I went on to tell him how I took the fish. Naturally, I gave him all the details. I told him which pool it was and where the fish was lying. I explained how I had happened to see the trout rise while looking at the stream from the road. I told him what fly I had tied on—

38

a No. 10, brown-and-white, Bi-visible—and I showed him just how I'd made my cast to avoid some hemlock branches. In doing so, of course, I raised my arm and made the proper gesture for a loop cast. Do you know just what a perfect loop cast should be?"

"Why, no, George, but—"

"Look!" said George. "Here's your fish." He laid a hastily gathered Gideon Bible on the bed. "Now, then, here's where your fly should light." He dented in the bedclothes with his thumb. "Please bear in mind that it's the leader, not the fly, that, as a rule arouses suspicion in a trout. That being so, how are we going to place the fly here with the fish here, and not let the leader—"

"George," I interrupted, "I'm going to ask you again to postpone any fishing experiences, any instructions as to the pursuit and capture of fish, to a more suitable hour and place."

George laid the book slowly back on the table from which he had taken it. He rubbed out the dent in the bedclothes. He eyed me silently for a moment and said at last, with a slight shrug of his shoulders, "Well, it takes all kinds of people to make a world."

"True," I agreed. "But after all, isn't that a blessing? What if we were all anglers? Think of the consequences to art, medicine, philosophy, business!"

"Business, hah!" said George bitterly. "Why bring that up? Well, anyway, I'll get on with what I've been telling you. As I said, I'd made the gesture for a loop cast. A moment later the pale young man interrupted me just as I was telling Woodruff what the fish had done after I'd hooked him. It seems I'd bid in something when I'd raised my arm. I told the pale young man there had been a mistake. He told me I had one of the greatest bargains of the sale. I said, 'I don't care how much of a bargain it is, I don't want it.' His eyebrows simply disappeared. He said, 'My dear sir, what do you think would happen to us if people made it a rule to come in here and bid in articles and then repudiate their bids?" Well, that did stump me for a minute, and his damned eyebrows got my goat, I suppose, because I told him I was not in the habit of repudiating anything, and asked him what he claimed I'd bought. He said, 'You have purchased an absolutely brand-new, golden-oak sideboard with heavy beveled mirror, for the ridiculous sum of twenty-six dollars.' I said, 'All right, here's your money,' and gave him my address. He thanked me and that settled that.

"I started in to finish telling Woodruff about the big rainbow, but he had disappeared. I was delighted, of course, but suddenly I wondered whether he had really left the place or taken another seat for some reason. I stood up to look around and see if I could locate him, and I got what will probably be the most fearful shock of my life. . . . I'm going to have a snifter before I tell you. Join me?"

"Not just yet, thanks."

George replenished his glass, sampled its contents and lit a cigarette.

"Any one might have expected what I discovered when I looked around that auction room," he told me through a cloud of smoke. "Any one that hadn't been turned into a plain dope by finding what I had stumbled across that day. You couldn't put up half a hundred kohinoors at auction and keep the business dark, now could you? Well, this was the same thing, only more so. The first thing I noticed was that the last three or four rows of camp chairs were filled with men with pipes in their mouths. Then I saw men with pipes simply massed at the back of the room. And then I got the shock I mentioned. Half the Anglers' Club of New York were there. And that wasn't a starter. There were men from dozens of other clubs —upstate, Jersey, Pennsylvania—I knew most of 'em. There was a lot of the crowd who put up at Keener's and fished the Big River from Roscoe down, and about as many more who stay at Phœnicia and fish the Esopus from the Reservoir up. They stood there not saying a word, not looking at one another—just staring straight ahead—waiting. My heart simply sank into my boots.

"In staring around, I noticed a woman— she was not a bad-looking woman—so my eyes came back to her automatically. I thought vaguely that I'd seen her somewhere before. Then she bowed to me. It was Grace Witherbee. To show you what can happen to a man's mind at a time like that, I remember wondering what she was doing there. That will give you a faint idea of the strain I was under.

"Just then a man sat down in the chair Woodruff had left. He got out a pipe and looked hard at me. Then he said, 'Hail, hail, the gang's all here! My name's Blodgett. Ever fish the Ausable?' I said, 'I have.' He said, 'Ever fish the Margaree in Nova Scotia?' I said, 'I have.' He said, 'Ever fish the Big Sturgeon in Michigan?' I said, 'I have.' He said, 'Ever fish the St. Margarite in Quebec?' I said, 'I have.' He said, 'Ever fish the Gunnison in Colorado?' I said, 'I have.' He said, 'Ever fish the Wahoohoo above Squidjum Lake?' I told him I had not. I told him I had never even heard of it.

"He said, 'Neither have I, brother. I was just putting the acid test on you.' Then he whacked me on the back and asked to see my catalogue. I gave it to him without a word. I had taken an instant dislike to the fellow. As he began to turn the pages he started in to tell me about losing a big salmon up on a Gaspé river. I stood it for some time and then interrupted him. I told him this was not a suitable occasion to listen to fishing exploits. I said my mind was too fully occupied with matters of the moment to profit by anything he might say. He slapped me on the back again, said, 'I get you,' and pointed to the Jenks' rods in the catalogue. Then he looked toward the back of the room and said, 'Boy,

44

we're as safe here as on a trench raid.' I made absolutely no reply of any sort. . . . Your glass has been empty for ten minutes. How about it?"

I hesitated and was lost.

"Make it a short one," I said.

With our glasses filled, George went on:

"I have had some trying experiences in my time," he confessed simply. "But for pure mental torture, nothing has ever equaled the sale that day of my old Spinozas. The auctioneer made a speech when he came to them. It was then I began to realize he was not the man I had taken him for. The speech was little short of pathetic. He said the late Andrew B. Jenks had been a celebrated fisherman—not angler—fisherman. He said the sale of his paraphernalia—think that over—'paraphernalia'—offered other fishers—get that—the chance of a lifetime. Mind you, he used the very phrase that had occurred to me, and I'm no word painter. It was—well, feeble, I felt, from him. Fifty

45

old Spinozas, and I had heard that auctioneer grow really eloquent over cracked dishes
and rickety furniture. He wound up by saying, 'I am now about to sell the collection of
that celebrated fisherman, the late Andrew
B. Jenks. Page 47 in your catalogues.'

"I was sitting there in a short silence that
followed. My heart had begun to pound like
fury, I remember, when the Blodgett fellow
said, 'Ever read his *Brown Trout of the
Pyrenees?*' I said, 'Whose, pray?' He said,
'Jenks'.' I told him I had not. Blodgett
said, 'Not so hot.' Then he slapped the
catalogue and said, 'But Andy had the tools.'
My dislike of him was increased by his flip-
pancy at such a time. I said, 'When you are
entirely through with my catalogue, I'd appreciate just a glance at it.' He said, 'Sure,
brother, I know 'em by heart, anyway.
There's a twelve-footer that I'm going to
wade through blood after.' I took the catalogue without a word.

"And now get this: The first thing put up

46

was a two-piece, seven-foot, two-ounce, dry-fly rod. A man stood on the platform next to the auctioneer's pulpit and waved it in the air in circles—in circles, mind you—and this is what that auctioneer said. He said, 'Now, then, what am I offered for the little fishing pole? Who'll start it at a dollar?' He called a fairy-weight Spinoza a fishing pole. I'm asking you to think that over—and, remember, I'd admired him.

"Well, there was an awful silence for a minute. Then a voice boomed out of the stillness—it was really terrific, everything being so quiet that way, after we'd been listening to the squeaks over doodads and what-nots that had been going on. The voice said, 'Listen, you; twenty-five dollars.' Another voice like a Jersey bull's said, 'That's getting him told. Thirty-five.' Now, that fairy weight had cost fifty dollars new. What do you suppose they took it up to?"

"I haven't an idea, George."

"Well, make a guess."

47

"Oh, forty-five dollars."

"If it didn't sell for seventy-five dollars, may I never step into a trout stream again. And listen; that auctioneer was just a spectator. He never opened his head. He just sat there with his mouth open until he finally said in a weak voice, 'Are you all through? Sold to the tall gentleman in the gray hat on the right.'

"The Blodgett fellow looked at me. I looked at him. He said, 'Get the cripples and children back of the ropes.' I said, 'This is an outrage. It's plain lunacy.' He said, 'If it wasn't for the depression, they'd use poison gas.' I remember feeling more warmly disposed towards him. I suppose it was because we were—well, fellow sufferers, if you get what I mean."

"Yes, George," I said.

"There is no need of going into the rest of it. It was all just as senseless, just as exasperating, as that first performance. One remarkable thing was that as it went on, I felt more and more drawn to Blodgett. After each rod sold for some stupefying figure, he'd never show that he was being cut to the quick. He'd give a sort of dry laugh he had and say something extraordinary. He must have been in the war, because his talk was like that. He'd say, 'Third platoon forward, and don't step on the wounded.' He'd say, 'Into the shell holes, men; it's shrapnel.' Once he said something I didn't understand. I don't think it had anything to do with the war. It was when two men started bidding on a rod after every one else had stopped. It was a sixteen-foot, wet-fly, salmon rod, and they took it above a hundred dollars. Blodgett said, 'It's better than a natural; it's a grudge scrap.' Now, what would you make of that?"

"I think it has to do with prize fighting," I said.

"I believe you're right," George agreed. "I remember, now, he added something about throwing science to the winds and slugging toe to toe. He was an unusual person. I admit that even though he did turn out to be a stubborn jackass."

"How, George?"

"I'll come to that presently. I want to tell you one thing that happened that threw a little more light on the auctioneer. That first rod had knocked him out of his stride, but he came back and took charge of the next sale. It wasn't long till he was handling everything like Mussolini again. He kept calling the rods 'poles,' but he'd start each one at twenty-five or thirty dollars and say that seventy-five dollars was just a fraction of what a rod was worth. Once Blodgett said, 'I'll bet he ate up the third grade. He's hell on fractions.'

"Well, anyway, at last the man on the platform began to wave a steel bait rod about. It cost three or four dollars new. I can't imagine why a man like Jenks should have had such a thing. The auctioneer simply rose up in his pulpit. He said, 'Now, gentlemen,

50

I have the privilege of offering you a steel fishing pole—think of it, gentlemen; a fishing pole of the finest compressed steel. Such a pole should last several lifetimes. What am I offered for the steel fishing pole? To be used and passed on to your grandchildren. Who'll start it at fifty dollars?' I give you my word, that's what he said. You could have heard a pin drop any place in the room. The crowd was simply stunned. The auctioneer said, 'Well, then, forty dollars?' No one said anything, of course. The auctioneer said, 'Thirty-five,' and waited. He said, 'Come, come, gentlemen. Make an offer.' There was another silence, and then a voice said, 'Fifty cents to get it out of the way, and you keep it for your own grandchildren.' "

George broke off and chuckled. "Not bad, if you ask me," he said. "You should have seen that auctioneer. It took all the Mussolini out of him. He said, 'I'm licked. I quit. Make your own prices, gentlemen.' "

George chuckled again, then suddenly sobered. "That was the only light moment of the rod sale. All the rest was just a sort of horrible nightmare, as far as I was concerned. You can understand that, after what I'd planned to do for Isabelle."

"Yes, George," I said, "but what about Blodgett disappointing you in the end?"

"Disappointing me!" George exclaimed. "Well, I hope so! I told you he proved to be a stubborn jackass. I'll tell you what happened and you can decide whether I've overstated it or not. You remember I'd looked at a dozen or so rods before the sale. Well, one of 'em had impressed me particularly. I had even noted its number in the catalogue. It was a twelve-foot, dry-fly, salmon rod that was just simply a poem. It was a two-handed rod—make no mistake about that—two-handed. Of course, there is a school of thought that's trying to foist single-handed, dry-fly, salmon rods on the anglers of this country, and what do you suppose they advo-

cate? They favor a longer butt that fits into
a hollow in the actual butt of the rod after
you hook your fish. Of all the cock-eyed
notions, that beats them all. In the first
place, a single-handed rod at the required
weight will simply break your wrist in two
before you've fished it half a day. In the
second place—"

"I know, George," I said, "but what about
Blodgett?"

"But you don't know," George informed
me heatedly. "You don't know the half of it.
You don't know a tenth of it. I haven't even
started to tell you. Why, I could keep giving
you reasons from now until morning, why
single-handed salmon rods, dry or wet, are
simply—"

"That's just it, George," I managed to
break in. "I couldn't possibly sit here until
morning. Get back to your friend Blodgett,
like a good fellow."

"Don't call him my friend," said George.
"Not after— Listen. I'd been sitting there

in a sort of torture chamber, watching my old Spinozas go, one after another. I'd make an extravagant bid on one now and then, but mere extravagance wouldn't get you a ferrule off one of those rods. If you wanted a rod you had to go hog wild.

"Well, they'd worked so far down the list of rods that I knew something had to be done or I'd walk out without one single old Spinoza to show for all my plans and the hours I'd spent there.

"I decided, finally, that I'd take home the twelve-foot salmon rod that I'd liked particularly, or bust a G string. When it came up, I let it go to forty dollars, and was about to bid when Blodgett, out of a clear sky, said, 'Fifty.' I thought, 'He doesn't know I want this rod,' so I gave him a friendly smile and said, 'Sixty.' He looked at me quickly. He didn't smile back. He said, 'Seventy.'

"I felt my earlier dislike of him begin to return. I gave him a look in which there was no smile, I assure you, and asked him, coldly, a point-blank question. I said, 'Why are you bidding?' He said, 'This is the baby I've been waiting for, major.' I said, 'I'll have to tell you I particularly want this rod.' Then I bid, 'Seventy-five.' Blodgett said, 'Eighty.' I said, 'Are you going to keep on with this?' Blodgett said, 'Report to G. H. Q. that we're holding our position in the face of heavy fire.' I bid eighty-five. Blodgett bid ninety. I bid ninety-five. Blodgett bid a hundred. For a moment I hesitated, I confess it. The rod cost seventy dollars new. Then I thought about Blodgett using, or rather misusing, that old Spinoza—casting short, sloppy casts with it, no doubt. Letting the fly and leader smack down on the water, in all probability. I turned and looked him in the eye and bid one hundred and twenty-five dollars in a loud, clear voice. Blodgett got up from his seat. He called out, 'Stretcher bearers, stretcher bearers!' and went out of the place with every one looking at him. Curious performance, wasn't it? His stubbornness cost me about fifty dollars."

George refreshed himself from his glass and went on.

"When all the rods and a lot of reels, lines, leader boxes, et cetera, had been sold, the gang paid at the cashier's window for what they'd bought and then made a bee line for the rug room to test their rods. I put mine together, tested it for a moment or so, and then started to show it to men I knew. Not a man was interested in my rod. They all, without a single exception, tried to get me to look at theirs. Extraordinary how self-centered most men are. Have you noticed it?"

"Well, yes, I come across it now and then," I confessed.

"I regret what followed," George went on. "I admit it frankly. It had a decided bearing on what finally happened to Isabelle and me. I feel certain that despite the strain I'd been under, I should have remembered

56

the purpose of my visit to the auction rooms shortly after the rod sale was over. As a matter of fact, I did remember eventually. It came to me with startling clearness. I'll get to that presently. The fact remains that my mind was confused, not to say numbed, by all that had happened. You can readily understand that. It was now further distracted in a quite unexpected manner.

"It seemed that Woodruff, whom I had encountered earlier that afternoon, had not left the auction room. He had remained for the sale and had bought a seven-and-a-half-foot, two-piece, three-ounce, dry-fly rod. He somehow conceived the idea of rigging the rod with a Vomber reel and a Gebhart tapered line, Size F, he had secured from the sale of tackle, and after tying on a leader and fly, standing at the edge of one rug and casting for a medallion in the center of another rug.

"Well, the idea took like wildfire. Presently it became a series of casting matches for a stake. Each man put a dollar in the pool. He was then allowed one cast. The best casts were marked on the rug with a piece of chalk. The nearest cast to the exact center of the medallion won the pool. You'd be surprised how absorbing those competitions became. Each pool contained about thirty dollars. Woodruff, I noticed, won most of them. I was not lucky enough to win a pool for some time. I had contributed twenty-two dollars, I remember, before I succeeded in winning. This left me eight dollars to the good. At that precise moment it came to me that I had to go back to the auction room to purchase the cupboard for Isabelle.

"I excused myself, returned to the auction room and was really startled to find that the cupboard had already been put up and sold. The thought occurred to me that if I could find the purchaser I might yet get the cupboard by offering an advance over the price paid.

Fatal Gesture

"I went to the cashier's window and asked for the name of the purchaser. The cashier referred to her slips and told me No. 827 had been sold to Mrs. Thomas H. Witherbee. She started to give me the address, but I told her it wasn't necessary, and asked to use the telephone. I called up the Witherbees', but Grace was out. I went home and called up again, and she had just returned. When she came to the phone, I explained what I wanted and asked her if she would take a very substantial advance over what she had paid, for the cupboard. This is what she said. She said, 'All the money you've got, George Potter, wouldn't buy that cupboard, and please tell Isabelle I said so.' Strange about women. Apaches aren't a marker to 'em.

"Well, I was pretty sick, after Grace tomahawked me that way, but just before dinner a truck drove up with the sideboard I'd bought. I'd forgotten the thing completely. I told them to put it in the breakfast room

and went in to look at it when it was un-
wrapped. I was worried, I admit that.
Naturally, I didn't want to disappoint Isabelle, even though I'd done everything hu-
manly possible to get the cupboard for her.
I was worried, as I say, until I got a look at
what I'd bought. Then I cheered up mighty
quick. The pale young man hadn't overstated it a particle. I want to tell you that
sideboard looked as though it had just come
from the factory. There wasn't a dent or a
scratch on it. It had a polish you could see
your face in. And the brass handles on the
drawers looked as though they'd never been
so much as touched. The beveled mirror
was there, just as the pale young man had
said, and it was a corker. Furthermore—
and now get this—the sideboard was yellow
—you'll remember how she had gone on
about the yellow shelves. It was just a happy
accident, I thought. I was just luckier than
I really deserved to be.

"When you consider what I'd been through

that day, I felt pretty good after dinner. Fact is, I was kind of anxious to have Isabelle get back and see what I'd bought her for twenty-six dollars, instead of her dilapidated cupboard. I got out my newest old Spinoza and put it together. I took it into the front hall where I'd have plenty of room to swing it.

"I was standing there testing the rod, when the front door opened. It was Isabelle. I hadn't expected her, of course. I thought for a minute that her sixth sense about rods had brought her all the way from New Rochelle to arrive just when I had it in the front hall. Well, naturally, I began to explain at once. I told her it was an old Spinoza. I said, 'Think of it—an old Spinoza, darling. They were selling them at that place you sent me to. Can you believe it?'

"She never even looked at the rod. She said, 'Oh, George, I've been perfectly awful. Mother had ptomaine poisoning.' I said,

'Well, darling, you didn't give it to her, did you?' Isabelle said, 'She's better, but I shouldn't have left her; I simply couldn't wait. Where is it?' I said, 'Where is what?' She said, 'Where is my cupboard—my Early American cupboard? Don't tell me it hasn't come yet. I couldn't bear it.' I said, 'Now, I'll explain about that, too, darling. There was a little slip.' I'll give you my word, she went as white as a sheet. She said, 'You didn't get it?' I said, 'I'm afraid I didn't, darling. Grace Witherbee beat me to the cupboard. But don't you worry. Don't you worry for a minute. I got something else.' She stood there just opening and closing her mouth in the queerest way. Then she said, 'George, not Grace Witherbee?' I said, 'Never mind her, darling, you wanted something yellow, didn't you? Well, that's exactly what I got, and not a scratch on it. It's in the breakfast room.'

"She went to the breakfast room without

a word. I took the rod down and followed her. When I got to the breakfast-room door, she was standing in front of the sideboard staring at it. I give you my word, she didn't look human. Her eyes seemed to be starting from her head. She was saying, 'Oh, God! Oh, God!' over and over again. And now listen carefully. Here is exactly what I said, no more and no less. I won't add or subtract one syllable. I said, 'Don't you like it, darling?' that's what I said. Is there anything in the slightest degree offensive in that question, I ask you?"

I was gripped by emotions too deep for utterance. I could only gaze at George and maintain a frozen silence.

"You needn't answer," said he. "Obviously not. And yet, those simple words unloosed on me such a tirade, such abuse, as I had never dreamed could pass a woman's lips." George ceased abruptly and dropped his head in his hands.

I waited for several moments.

63

"After all," I offered at last, "mere words aren't to be weighed against ten years of—er—devotion."

George raised his head and looked at me with bloodshot, haggard eyes.

"Mere words!" he said. "Do you know what she called me?"

"No, George, I don't, but—"

"I'll say you don't, and you never will—she was once my wife. But I'll say this much: I don't yet know where she ever learned such words. I can't yet understand how a girl of breeding—a girl who had led a sheltered life —ever heard such appalling epithets, let alone use them."

"But after all, George," I said, "this is a modern age. Women are no longer helpless, overly nice creatures. You must consider that when—"

George held up his hand to stop me.

"Useless," he said, with quiet dignity. "Absolutely useless. I appreciate your motives, but—" He broke off, regarded me cautiously for a moment, looked around the room as though to assure himself that no possible eavesdropper shared our privacy, then, "Listen," he said hoarsely, "you don't know everything yet."

"Is there more?"

"More? You haven't heard anything. I thought I wouldn't tell you. As I've already said, she was once my wife. Naturally I don't like to blacken her character beyond a certain point. But, after all, facts are facts. We've got to admit that."

"Yes, George, but don't tell me anything you don't care to."

"H-m-m," said George doubtfully. He got up, paced the room nervously for a moment, took a drink and returned to the bed. "I think I'll tell you," he said at last. "I owe it to myself."

"All right," I said. "Go ahead!"

George unconsciously lowered his voice and went on.

"I was standing there simply stupefied by

65

the things she was saying—simply stupefied. She kept it up until she ran out of breath. Then she began to stare at the sideboard again. She seemed to be looking at the mirror. She said, 'It isn't possible! It just isn't possible!' Suddenly, without the slightest warning, she snatched the middle joint of the rod from my hand and crashed it with all her strength into the sideboard mirror. Can you conceive of such a wanton, such a monstrous, act? Now can you?"

George rose and again took to pacing the floor. "Unbelievable!" he muttered, mopping his brow. "And yet I saw it with my own eyes. The middle joint of an old Spinoza!"

"Did it break the mirror?" I asked innocently, after giving him time to control his feelings.

George halted in his stride and whirled upon me.

"The mirror!" he roared. "Do you suppose I looked at the damn mirror? She broke the rod joint in two about three inches below the upper ferrule. Of course that ended our married life." He sank down on the bed and again buried his head in his hands.

"George," I said after a silence, "time works wonders. Just now you feel——"

"Don't talk about time," said George. "Do you think any man could ever forgive such willful, wicked, inhuman destruction? Never mind what she called me. Let that go. Just take the breaking of that middle joint—nothing else. Why, it will be years before I can bring myself to see her again, let alone——"

The telephone bell exploded suddenly within the narrow confines of those four drab walls. George leaped from the bed to the instrument as though galvanized.

"Hello," I heard. "Yes, Isabelle, this is George. . . . Oh, darling, not really! . . . Oh, darling, so am I! . . . Will I? In twenty minutes. Maybe fifteen."

67

George hung up abruptly, turned and dove under the bed for his bag.

"Lonesome!" he shouted at me. "Lonesome! What do you know about that?"

In not over one minute from the end of that telephone conversation between husband and wife I found myself alone. I had become the sole occupant of the late sleeping quarters of George Baldwin Potter. The neckties, I noticed, were gone. The empty dresser missed those warming bits of color. I recalled seeing the ends of several of them trailing from a closed traveling bag as it was borne, like a hurricane, toward the elevator.